nickelodeon™

BUBBLE GUPPIES™

FIREFIGHTER GIL!

Adapted by Mary Tillworth
Based on the teleplay "Firefighter Gil to the Rescue!" by Clark Stubbs
Illustrated by Paul E. Nunn

A Random House PICTUREBACK® Book

Random House 🏠 New York

Early one morning, Molly and Gil were on their way to school with Bubble Puppy. Suddenly, a squirrel jumped out of the bushes.

"Arf! Arf!" barked Bubble Puppy. He ran after the squirrel and chased it up a tree. But then he couldn't get down!

Gil climbed up to help Bubble Puppy. When he looked down, he got really dizzy. Gil was stuck, too!

A fire truck raced over to the tree, and a firefighter got out. He called to his partner to raise the ladder, and then he climbed up and rescued Gil and Bubble Puppy!

"Thanks for saving us!" Gil said to the firefighter. Bubble Puppy barked happily. Gil noticed that the firefighter had a dog, too.

"This is Dotty. She's our fire dog!" said the firefighter.

After the fire truck left, Molly, Gil, and Bubble Puppy continued on their way to school.

"I can't wait to tell everyone about getting rescued by a real firefighter!" said Gil.

In the classroom, Gil and Molly told Mr. Grouper and their friends about their adventure. "I just got rescued by a firefighter! Bubble Puppy and I were stuck in a tree, and he saved us!" Gil said.

"Yeah!" said Molly. "He raised the ladder and climbed way up high to help!"

"Sounds like a real emergency!" exclaimed Mr. Grouper.
"What's an emergency?" Oona asked.
"An emergency is when someone needs help right away," answered Nonny.

Gil thought the firefighter was totally awesome.
He wanted to be a firefighter, too! "What does a
firefighter do?" he asked Mr. Grouper.

"Let's find out," said Mr. Grouper. "Line up, everybody! We're going to the fire station!"
"Field trip!" the Bubble Guppies cheered.

When the Bubble Guppies and Mr. Grouper arrived at the fire station, they saw a fire truck outside. It had a long ladder and a shiny siren.

"A fire truck has everything you need in an emergency,"
Mr. Grouper explained as everyone gathered around.
"Let's take a look!"

"When firefighters get to an emergency, they might need to rescue someone way up high. That means they'll have to climb a ladder," said Mr. Grouper.

Gil and Molly watched as a firefighter raised the long ladder into the air.

"And if firefighters have to put out a fire, they use a hose," continued Mr. Grouper.

A firefighter attached a hose to a fire hydrant, and water gushed out.

"When there's an emergency, a fire truck turns on its siren. The bright lights and loud sound tell everyone to move out of the way so the firefighters can do their job," Mr. Grouper explained.

The Bubble Guppies started home from the station. "Firefighters are the coolest! I want to be a firefighter!" exclaimed Gil.

Just then, they saw a fire truck on the road with its lights flashing. The siren blared. There was an emergency!

Gil and Molly followed the fire truck to the emergency. Dotty and some firefighters were stuck! Dotty had chased a squirrel into a tree. When the firefighters tried to rescue her, their ladder had broken.

"This is a job for
Firefighter Gil!" Gil said.

Gil went into the fire truck and put on a fire hat and coat. He bravely climbed up the ladder. But it wasn't long enough! Gil pulled a walkie-talkie out of his coat. "We need to make the ladder taller!" he told Molly.

Molly nodded and pulled the lever that raised the ladder.

The ladder got taller and taller. Putting one hand over the other, Gil climbed the last few rungs—and reached the firefighters and Dotty! Gil had saved the day!

They all climbed down the ladder
until they were safely on the ground.
"*Arf! Arf!*" barked Dotty.
"She's saying thank you,"
a firefighter told Gil with a smile.

"Hooray for Firefighter Gil!" everyone cheered.